The Spark Files

Terry Deary trained as an actor before turning to writing full-time. He has many successful fiction and non-fiction children's books to his name, and is rarely out of the best-seller charts.

Barbara Allen trained and worked as a teacher and is now a full-time researcher for the Open University.

The Spark Files

Book Four

Bat and Bell

illustrated by Philip Reeve

faber and faber

First published in 1998
by Faber and Faber Limited
3 Queen Square London WC1N 3AU

Typeset by Faber and Faber Ltd
Printed in England by Mackays of Chatham plc, Chatham, Kent

© Terry Deary and Barbara Allen, 1998
Illustrations © Philip Reeve, 1998

Cover design: Shireen Nathoo

Terry Deary and Barbara Allen are hereby identified as authors
of this work in accordance with Section 77 of the Copyright,
Designs and Patents Act 1988

A CIP record for this book
is available from the British Library

ISBN 0-571-19371-4

10 9 8 7 6 5 4 3 2 1

For my daughter, Siân, with love. BA

Bat and Bell

File 1

Sally Spark (Moi!)

Probably the cleverest girl in
Duckpool School. I'm the sort of girl
teachers love to have in their class.
I probably know more than they do!

Sally Spark is my name
Being brainy is my game
There may be a one who's
                        better

But, you know, I've never met her!

File 2

Susie Spark
(kid sister)

Being a female, and my sister,
is a great start in life for this child.
One day she may be almost as good as
me!

Sister Sue is so neat
She's a caring child... that's
                          sweet
Fighting for the poor and weak
Susie has a real tough streak.

File 3

Granny Spark

     A wise old head on wise old
shoulders and a wise (but skinny) body...
all held up on knobbly knees.

Granny Spark is a winner
Shows us all there's life left in her
Never tired and never cross,
In the house she's quiet - but
                      boss.

File 4

Sam
and Simon Spark.

Simon (Susie's twin) and
Sam, our evil, twisted, ugly and smelly
brothers. They're just so, so, so...
BOYISH!

Sam and Simon are no good
How could these two share our
blood?

Football, football, is their game
Like a football, they've no brain!

File 5

Councillor
Tripewell.

Fat, bald and sweaty. This
man is our local councillor because
people are too scared to vote for his
opponents

"Tripewell, tripe-smell, makes his
                                        pies
Out of dead sheep guts and
                                   eyes."
That's what kids sing in our
                                  school
Trouble is... I think it's true!

Chapter 1

This is a terrifying tale of bats and bloodsuckers, a haunted graveyard and a phantom bell that strikes thirteen. This tale will freeze your blood colder than a polar bear's bum.

Spark file health warning:
Do not read this book in the dark with the lights out!

It is also a tale of two rats. A couple of two-legged rats called Simon Spark and Sam Spark. My brothers. It all began with their jokes . . .

THERE WERE TWO FLIES PLAYING FOOTBALL IN A SAUCER. ONE FLY SAID TO THE OTHER FLY, "WE'D BETTER PLAY BETTER THAN THIS NEXT WEEK – WE'RE IN THE CUP!

AND THERE WERE TWO EARWIGS ON THE WAY TO THE CUP FINAL. THEY WERE SINGING "EARWIG-GO, EARWIG-GO, EARWIG-GO!"

I didn't say they were *good* jokes, did I? Just the sort of silliness that pathetic boys like Simon and Sam *would* come up with. They were supposed to be doing homework, like I was.

'What are you two so happy about?' I asked.

'The new soccer stadium down the road,' Sam grinned.

'We don't have a new soccer stadium down the road,' I pointed out as I worked at my computer on the dining-room table.

'Hah!' Simple Simon said. 'For once you are wrong, Miss Smartie-knickers-Sally! Screw your spectacles on to your eyeballs and grab a squint of this.' (Sometimes my brother's crude talk makes me ashamed to be in the same family.)

He thrust the evening paper under my nose. I placed it on the table between me and my sister Susie and we read it.

DUCKPOOL DAILY POST

14 October   Price:Only 30p

Super Stadium Sited on Stagnant Swamp

Today Oldcastle United supporters got the news they have been waiting to hear. They will be getting a new super soccer stadium in time for next season.

Wasteland District Council have agreed to sell the boggy ground known as Duckpool Swamp to the football club.

Duckpool councillor Timothy Tripewell (51) said today, 'It will bring thousands of supporters into the area. Duckpool shops will be little goldmines and local people won't have to travel so far to see their favourite team. Anyway, that swamp is an eyesore and it would have cost us thousands of pounds to tidy up.'

Councillor Tripewell, who owns Duckpool's biggest

pie shop, said, 'The football club are over the moon.' Oldcastle United chairman, V Donald Racula, was interviewed last night in the

graveyard overlooking Duckpool Swamp. 'A major project like this brings new blood into a dying community,' he said.

The Duckpool Daily Post, as usual, is first with this exciting news. In the words of Oldcastle fans, 'We'll support you evermore!'

'Your grandad will be pleased,' Gran said suddenly. 'A great supporter of the Canaries, your grandad.'

'Why are Oldcastle United called the Canaries?' Simon asked.

Gran sighed. 'The great enemy are Lanchester City. They wear red and they're known as the Robins. Oldcastle *don't* wear red so they call themselves the Canaries, see?'

'Oldcastle United wear black and white stripes! You don't see many black and white striped canaries,' Sam objected.

'Aha!' Gran cried. 'And you don't see any red ones either, that's what Grandad told me!'

Susie and I looked at her. Worried. 'Grandad's been dead twenty years, Gran,' Susie said.

Gran blinked her blue eyes behind the glass of her little round spectacles. 'He's buried in the churchyard right next to the swamp. Now he can be there in spirit . . . if you see what I mean.'

That was seriously spooky and I shuddered. I tugged at Susie's sleeve and led her into the quiet of the kitchen. When we were sitting at the kitchen table I asked, 'Why is no one trying to stop this stadium?'

'It'll bring a lot of money to Duckpool,' Susie shrugged.

'It'll bring a lot of money to people like Councillor Tripewell,' I said. 'It'll ruin one of the last wetland areas in the region. We did a school project there last year. It's full of newts and frogs and marshland grasses . . .'

'And old supermarket trollies and rusty bikes and dead sofas,' she reminded me.

'But it isn't *dead*! They're calling it "stagnant" and it's *not*!' I cried. 'We need a campaign to save it!'

'Yes,' Susie nodded and her eyes glowed. I knew she liked that kind of thing – she'd tried hard: *Friends of the Snail* (no one would shell out for that), *Action for the Improvement of School Dinners* (that got her banned from Duckpool School dining hall) and *Society for the Preservation of the Dinosaur* (that soon died out).

It was her spelling that let her down in the end. They scratched their heads when she marched round the playground with a banner saying 'Save Wales'. They laughed when her posters said, 'Champagne for clean hair!' when she wanted a *campaign* for clean *air*.

'We need to test the water in the swamp, to prove it's still fresh,' I said eagerly.

'How do we do that, Sally?' she asked.

'Fetch me a red cabbage from the vegetable rack,' I ordered. As she reached for it I took a booklet from my school bag.

EARTH WARRIOR

SAVE YOUR PLANET FOR A RAINY DAY

I turned to the page we needed . . .

Testing for acid water
Acid in your local water supply can kill off plants,
fish and other water creatures. Test it now using this
home-made 'indicator'.
Chop up about a quarter of a red cabbage
Put the pieces into a saucepan and add enough
boiling water to cover the cabbage
Stir and leave to soak for 20 minutes
Strain the liquid into a bottle. This is your 'indicator'.
Keep it in the fridge.

We'd just finished making our liquid when the kitchen door opened and our rat-like brothers stood there. 'What are you two up to?' Simon demanded.

'SOS!' Susie said.

'Save Our Souls?' Sam asked, puzzled.

'Save Our Swamp,' I told them.

The boys looked at one another. 'Oh really?' Simon said. And I didn't like the way their little noses curled back. Give them a set of whiskers and they'd have looked just like the rats they were.

Chapter 2

Susie and I decided to test the water in the swamp after school the next day.

'I think we should wait until it gets dark,' I said. 'We don't want anyone working out what we're doing.'

After tea the boys came downstairs with black and white scarves round their necks and turned up the sound on the television when the local news came on . . .

SO THE QUESTION ON EVERYONE'S EARS IS... WHO'S GOING TO WIN TONIGHT GLEN?

ER, WELL, IF YOU ASK ME I THINK IT'LL BE A TIGHT GAME AND EITHER OLDCASTLE OR LANCHESTER WILL WIN. UNLESS IT'S A DRAW, OF COURSE. BUT I'M PREDICTING A WIN FOR THE CANARIES!

AND THE SCORE?

NIL-NIL

THERE YOU HAVE IT, STRAIGHT FROM THE HORSE'S TAIL. GLEN HODDLE TIPS OLDCASTLE TO WIN BY THE NARROWEST OF MARGINS. NOW IT'S BACK TO THE STUDIO FOR A REPORT OF VAMPIRES SEEN IN A DUCKPOOL GRAVEYARD

IT'S KEN GODDLE ACTUALLY...

ER... WHAT? SORRY! VAMPIRES SEEN IN A KEN GODDLE GRAVEYARD... EH?

The boys started chanting a few mindless football songs as they left the house – they didn't have to try very hard to be mindless, but it was tough trying to make, 'We love you Oldcastle United, we do!' fit the tune.

When the house went quiet I said, 'Time for homework.'

'Why have you got your coat on?' Gran asked.

'I've got to do some bark rubbings for Art,' I answered. 'There's an interesting old tree by the swamp.'

'Why has Susie got *her* coat on?'

'I need someone to hold the tree.'

We were about to walk out of the house when Gran started to put on her coat. For a horrible minute I thought she was going to come with us.

'Time to say goodnight to grandad and check he's looking tidy,' she said, tying her scarf on over her hat. She opened the front door. 'I'll just be over the wall from you,' she said quietly. 'It's not so safe at night as it was when I were a lass.' When we reached the church she slipped through the great iron gates.

'Have you got the bottle of indicator from the fridge?' I asked Susie.

'Yes and the jam jar and string for taking the water sample,' she replied.

It was getting quite dark by the time we reached the old tree at the edge of the swamp below the graveyard wall. It was a black, dead tree, with a twisted trunk and bent as a vulture's neck.

I don't know why people are always scared of graveyards. What can possibly be in there to hurt you? But even I shivered a little when I heard two people talking behind the graveyard wall. A bat flew overhead, just a ragged silhouette against the full moon.

We leaned over the swamp and peered at the water. It looked clear enough to me. True there was a lot of rubbish around the swamp but the water looked fairly pure in the silver light.

'Right, Susie, you know what you're doing. Get on with it,' I said. 'I've written down the instructions here,' I added.

I passed her the paper.

Testing Water for acid.

1. Dip jam jar into pond to collect water. **DO NOT** fall in.

2. Pour some of the indicator into the pond water.

3. Wait an hour or two.

4. If it's polluted then it will be more acid than it should be. The mixture will turn pink after you've added the indicator.

'What will *you* be doing, Sally?' Susie asked me.

'I'm supposed to be doing some bark rubbings so I'd better have some when we go home.'

Susie scurried round to the other side of the dead tree while I got on with the bark rubbings.

After a few minutes I heard a sharp crack and Susie came creeping back looking a bit shaken. 'Cor, that was close,' she said.

'Did someone see you?' I asked.

'No, I nearly fell in.'

'How?'

'I held on to a branch while I leaned over the pond. The thing's rotten!' she explained.

As we started to walk home I heard the crack of a twig. It was probably a cat hunting for food. When we turned the corner into Shave Close I'm sure I heard footsteps behind us. I looked round, but there was no one to be seen.

We arrived home just before Gran and hid the jam jar in our bedroom.

'You meet some lovely people at the graveyard,' Gran said as she sat down at the kitchen table and took off her hat. 'I met a really nice man with lovely shiny black hair – looked just like a film star with that long flowing cape, and his bow tie. He was ever so interested in how many people come and visit the graves.'

'Why would he want to know that?' Susie wondered.

'Maybe he'd open a pie shop if there's enough people interested. I'd enjoy sharing a corned-beef pasty with your grandad. Of course, I had to tell him, it's really only me and Mrs Grimley that visit the graveyard.'

'Why would you tell grandad that?' I asked.

'*No!* I told the man in the black suit! I said, poor

Martha Grimley doesn't get out much now she's under the doctor with her leg. And I told him how excited Grandad and I are about the new football stadium. He said he liked football.'

'I'm not sure you should be talking to strange men in graveyards, Gran,' I said. 'Especially with this story of a vampire in the news.'

She blinked. 'It's odd how a man that well-dressed should have such terrible false teeth,' she sighed.

'Pointed fangs!' Susie squeaked. 'Ooooh! Gran!'

I heard the boys return. They weren't singing now. I thought it was perhaps because Oldcastle United had lost.

In my bedroom Susie and I took out the jam jar and the indicator from under my bed. The pond water had stayed the same colour. I was right! The water wasn't polluted the way Councillor Tripewell tried to make out.

Now for the next stage of our plan to save the swamp.

Chapter 3

Next morning at seven I picked up the phone and called the local television station. 'Get me the Controller of Programmes!' I ordered.

'Would that be Controller of Programmes in-brackets-*News-And-Current-Affairs*-close-brackets or the Controller of Programmes in-brackets-*Entertainment-and-Sport*-close-brackets?' the operator asked.

'In-brackets-*News*-close-brackets,' I told her. 'This is the biggest news story to hit Duckpool since the Romans invaded.'

'Ooooh! I don't remember seeing that on *Tonight At Six*,' she said. 'I'd better put you through.'

The Controller could smell a good story. 'Tell me 'bout it, kid,' he said. I could picture him – smooth-haired, fat and chewing on a cigar.

'We're the SOS group!'

'The SAS! You're planning to invade? My secretary said something about some Romans were planning a big hit on the town.'

'S . . . O . . . S!' I said carefully. 'Save Our Swamp. It's a *great* story. Big business trying to murder poor little frogs. All that stands between their bulldozers and innocent tadpoles are two brave girls!'

'These Romans are invading in bulldozers? You sure you don't mean *tanks*?' he asked.

'It's about greedy Councillor Tripewell,' I said. 'He's claiming the swamp is stagnant . . . but we can prove it's clean!'

The Controller's voice changed. 'Hey! I know that Tripewell guy. Straight as a boomerang! If we could get a line on him it would be dynamite!'

At that moment Sam stuck his head over the banisters and looked down into the hall where I grasped the phone . . .

Sam ducked back into his bedroom to wake the other sleeping beauty, Simon. Breakfast was a quiet meal – unless you count the noises Simple Simon makes with crunchy cornflakes. I snapped on the radio.

AND IN SPORT YESTERDAY, OLDCASTLE UNITED LOST FIVE-NIL TO GREAT RIVALS LANCHESTER CITY. MANAGER KEN GODDLE SAID "WE WAS LUCKY TO GET NIL! THE LADS IS SICK AS A HERD OF PARROTS. PROMOTION TO THE PREMIER LEAGUE DON'T LOOK LIKELY THIS YEAR. WE WAS MORE RUBBISH THAN THE TOWN TIP!

Simon switched the radio off angrily and turned to Sam. 'They lost, then,' he groaned. 'Let's go to school,' he said.

'At this time of the morning?' Sam gasped. 'We'll be there before eight!'

'We can have a game of footie in the yard,' he said fiercely. 'Let's GO!'

Sam shrugged, said, 'Goodbye, Gran,' and trailed out of the door after Simon.

Gran picked up their half-empty plates. 'Waste of good food,' she muttered. 'When I were a lass . . . I were your age!'

Susie helped Gran wash the breakfast dishes – it was our turn this morning – while I phoned the local newspaper and radio station. Neither was interested in Save Our Swamp . . . until I mentioned the magic words . . .

COUNCILLOR TRIPEWELL!

. . . then both said they'd have reporters there for eight.

Ten minutes later I'd collected the jam jar with acid indicator in it. That would look good on television. 'The colours won't show up so well on the radio,' Gran warned me as we walked out of the door for our appointment with Fame!

The air was chilly and calm. Susie looked across the swamp and smiled. 'Lovely! That rainbow of colours on the water. Just like the rainbow after Noah's Ark landed.'

My heart stopped and my mouth went dry. I followed her gaze. There was certainly a dazzling pattern of every colour on the surface – but fresh water never looked like that. I dipped a finger in and sniffed. Oil! Someone had poured oil into the swamp!

'Excuse me! Are you the SAS?' a woman asked. Men trailed behind her with cameras and cables and microphones as more cars arrived with tape recorders and reporters.

'S . . . O . . . S,' I said. I was numb. This was a disaster. It called for quick thinking and a sharp brain. Luckily I have one.

Someone stuck a microphone under my nose and the woman said, 'Tell me, Sally, why do you want to save this polluted old swamp?'

I switched on my brightest smile and said, 'Not *polluted*! Just a little surface oil!'

'You wouldn't catch me swimming in it,' a reporter sneered.

'But oil is just on the top. Look . . . I'll show you!'

And I gave a demonstration just like a star television presenter . . .

FOR THIS EXPERIMENT WE NEEDED A GLASS OF WATER, AN EMPTY FILM CONTAINER ON A PIECE OF STRING, A FEW NUTS, BOLTS AND WASHERS AND A ¼ CUP OF COOKING OIL.

1 I FILLED THE GLASS FULL OF WATER AND POURED THE OIL INTO THE GLASS. YEUCH!

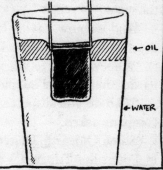

2 I PLACED THE CONTAINER ON THE SURFACE AND HELD IT UPRIGHT BY THE STRING. THEN I WEIGHED IT DOWN WITH THE BOLTS UNTIL THE TOP WAS JUST BELOW THE SURFACE OF THE OIL AND LET IT FILL...

← OIL

← WATER

3 I POURED THE LIQUID OUT OF THE CONTAINER AND REPEATED THIS. WOULD YOU BELIEVE IT? THE WATER WAS CLEAR! COOL OR WHAT?

AND HERE'S ONE I CLEANED EARLIER!

I used the jam jar we had with us. It wasted the indicator sample, but the demonstration was a sensation and the cameras caught it all. 'How did you do that?' a reporter asked.

'Oil is the easiest pollution to clear up,' I said with a satisfied grin. 'Whoever poured oil in here last night didn't know that. It floats on the surface and doesn't mix with the water.'

'And we now have a lovely clean swamp that doesn't deserve to die!' Susie put in passionately.

'Whoever tried to wreck our campaign will have to try harder than that!' I laughed.

'Who do you suspect?' the woman from the television company asked.

'Some Oldcastle United supporters who are in favour of Councillor Tripewell's plan!' I cried.

Then there came a soft but deadly voice from behind the crowd of reporters. 'Thank you for calling this little meeting,' Councillor Tripewell said. 'It gives me the chance to put the Oldcastle point of view.'

His bald, sweating head glistened in the morning sun and his gooseberry eyes glared at Susie and me. He stood in front of us and turned to the cameras. His voice was as oily as the stuff we'd cleaned off the water. 'Now it's time for the *truth*,' he said.

Chapter 4

The reporters turned their microphones towards Councillor Tripewell. The video camera operators jostled with the photographers to get a good picture.

Sally nudged me, 'How did he know there was going to be a press conference?'

'Spies in our midst,' I muttered.

The bald beast started to speak. 'I am delighted to be able to announce the plans we have for this wonderful site.'

'We know. You're going to build a football stadium,' a reporter said.

'Yes indeed. A great football stadium for a great team.'

'They weren't very great last night,' someone said and everyone laughed.

Tripewell glared at the man and continued, 'The stadium is only part of the plan. We aren't just building a stadium but will include an education centre that will concentrate on improving our environment. We feel it is important that our children are aware of the many problems that our planet faces.'

'Like destroying wildlife sites,' Susie murmured.

Tripewell went on, 'This will be a centre of excellence where children can come and study the glories of nature. They will have the use of all the facilities in the education centre and also the stadium.'

'This could be really good, Sally,' Susie said. 'It's just what we need.'

'Whose side are you on?' I hissed.

She turned red and looked at her shoes. They needed cleaning. I looked around at the people all listening to the councillor. Then I noticed a man walking towards the graveyard. I nudged Susie, 'See that man in a donkey jacket?'

'I didn't know donkeys wore jackets,' she gasped.

I gritted my teeth. 'Gran told us that no one visits the graveyard. But look, Susie!' This time she saw him. Meanwhile Councillor Tripewell was doing a wonderful job. I could see the headlines . . .

CARING COUNCILLOR'S DUCKPOOL DREAM

Reporters wept tears of joy as Duckpool's dearest Councillor announced his plans for a nature study centre at the new Stadium of Sun. 'This will be the greatest nature resource since Noah's Ark steamed over the waters of the world,' terrific Tripewell said today. 'Duckpool will lose one grubby little bog and gain an education centre second to none. The stadium will take up all the room, of course, but if there is a broom cupboard that is not in use we will hand it over – for a very small rent – to the local school as a nature centre.'

'What has Duckpool done to deserve such a wonderful man?' the reporters cried between cheers. What indeed!

The thought made me sick . . . so I stopped thinking and started listening.

'When can we see the plans for the centre?' a reporter shouted.

'What sort of things will be in the centre?' another called.

I looked towards the graveyard again and the man had disappeared but I could see Gran walking towards us.

'I'm glad you asked me about the centre,' said Councillor Tripewell. 'Children love studying animals. They can make a wormery like the one I have here.' He bent down and picked up an old fish bowl filled with mud. 'No one is a greater lover of nature than me. I find it very relaxing to keep a wormery on my office desk. I've had this leaflet run off that tells you how to make one.'

I grabbed a copy as they were passed around.

Making a Wormery

You need:

A big jar or small goldfish bowl, white paper, large elastic band, soil, sand (silver sand is best) leaves and earthworms.

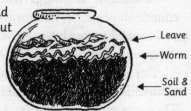

1. Put layers of soil and sand in the bowl until it is about two thirds full.

Leave

Worm

Soil & Sand

2. Put in the earthworms.

3. Next put in the leaves.

4. Make some holes in the paper so the worms get air and put it over the bowl. Hold it in place with an elastic band.

Remember to talk to your worms every day. Watch how busy they are. Looking at my worms reminds me that we humans must look after all the animals and plants on our planet. We must save the frogs, toads and newts in our ponds. And I mean that most sincerely.

Gran pushed her way through the reporters. 'What are you doing here?' I asked her.

'Thought I'd come and say good morning to Grandad before I did my shopping,' she said. 'What's going on?'

'Councillor Tripewell has announced plans to build an education centre in the new football stadium. He says we must look after animals.'

'Does he now?' she said mysteriously.

'If you have any more questions then just phone my secretary,' the councillor finished before he walked off towards the graveyard.

'Come on, Susie, let's follow him,' I said.

'Why?' she asked.

'I don't believe his story about the education centre. It just doesn't feel right,' I answered.

'Don't be late for tea,' Gran said. 'It's toad in the hole tonight – that's sausages in a batter pudding, of course. Not *real* toads! Heh! Heh! Heh!'

We ran from the swamp edge and hid behind the graveyard wall as near as we could to Councillor Tripewell.

'So how long do you think it will take to clear all these graves?' we heard him ask.

'Shouldn't take long with a bulldozer,' a man replied. 'There's only one old biddy that comes here to visit, Mr Racula says.'

'It'll make an excellent car park for the stadium,' Tripewell said. 'We'll start as soon as we get planning permission.'

I looked at Susie. They were going to put a car park on top of Grandad! How were we going to break the dreadful news to Gran?

'Did you hear all that?' Gran whispered in my ear.

My heart leapt into my mouth with fright. 'Why are you sneaking around?' I asked.

'I knew that Tripewell was up to something. The only animals his family have ever liked are the ones they put in their pies,' she said.

'What are we going to do?' I asked.

'We need a plan. You can start by getting all the support you can from your school mates. No one will listen to a wrinklie like me. I'll talk to you tonight.'

Susie and I turned towards school when Gran called, 'And remember . . . not a word of this to Grandad. If he finds out that they're planning to build a car park on top of him, he'll turn in his grave.'

Chapter 5

Tripewell was moving fast and we had to stop him. At morning break we called an emergency meeting of the SOS group and invited new members. Fifty people signed our petition to give us their support. We decided to take it to the town council and stop them giving permission.

To my surprise Sam and Simon were at the meeting. I wondered if they were to blame for the graffiti . . .

We, the young people of Duckpool, wish to oppose a new football stadium on the site of our swamp. Please don't spoil it for our children and their children!

Signed:

Sally Spark	Granny Spark
Suzie Spark	Harvey Quirke
Myrtle Brick	Sharon Pooter
ELViS SMiTH	Katie MacCallum
Tracey Crisp	James MacCallum
"We are not amused" signed Her Royal Highess Queen Victoria.	
Save our tadpoles - Signed FREDDIE THE FROG	

I waved the sheet under Simon's ratty nose. 'Know anything about this?'

'It's a forgery,' he said. 'I know for a fact there was no queen and no frog at the meeting.' Then he walked away laughing.

Everyone else agreed to take a blank sheet and go round the streets that night collecting signatures. But when we got home that evening and switched on the radio there was a shock in store . . .

AND NOW SOME GOOD NEWS AT LAST FOR OLDCASTLE UNITED'S TROUBLED TEAM. AFTER A THRASHING AT THE HANDS OF LANCHESTER LAST NIGHT THEY HAVE HEARD THEY WILL BE GETTING A NEW GROUND NEXT SEASON. IT WILL BE BUILT ON THE DERELICT SITE OF THE POLLUTED DUCKPOOL SWAMP...

THEY HAVEN'T GOT PERMISSION

WASTELAND DISTRICT COUNCIL HAD AN EMERGENCY MEETING OF THE PLANNING COMMITTEE THIS AFTERNOON AND GRANTED PERMISSION TO MR V. DONALD RACULA OF OLDCASTLE UNITED TO DRAIN THE SWAMP. IT IS BELIEVED THE GRAVEYARD ITSELF WILL BE COVERED IN CONCRETE TO BUILD A CAR PARK FOR THE STADIUM...

Gran was grim. 'They'll build that car park over my dead body,' she said.

'Hah!' Simon laughed. 'They'll build it over *Grandad's* dead body, that's for sure!' he said then ran out of the house with a football under his arm to play in the park.

Gran shook her head and said, 'When I were a lass that weren't a swamp. That were a *pool*. In fact that were the pool that gave Duckpool its name!'

'Do the newspapers know that?' Susie asked excitedly. 'Destroying the place that gave us our name. Taking the Pool out of Duckpool!'

'Yeah!' I agreed. 'It's like taking the Ham out of Nottingham!'

'You're left with Notting!' Susie nodded.

'Or taking the Gin out of Elgin.'

'You're left with an El of a place!'

'Take the Wick out of Warwick!'

'That would mean War!'

'Take the Folk out of Folkstone,' Gran muttered. 'And what have you got? An empty town!'

I thought she might be missing the point. 'So what happened to the pool, Gran?'

'Human beings happened,' she said. 'When I were at school we used the pool to study something called the Food Chain.' Gran sat at the table and used the computer art program to draw it for us.

'So what went wrong?' I asked.

'In the war we were short of food. We shot all the ducks and ate them!'

'Poor things,' Susie said.

'We were hungry, lass. We couldn't go to a shop and buy duck-flavoured crisps like you can nowadays!'

'Can you?' I asked. Gran ignored the question.

THE FOOD CHAIN OF THE DUCK POOL

① WATER COLLECTS → ② PLANTS GROW IN THE WATER

③ DUCKS, FISH AND FROGS FEED OFF THE PLANTS

④ HUMANS FEED OFF THE DUCKS

'With no fish to eat the plants, the weeds just took over and turned it into an overgrown swamp,' Gran said. 'You see. Nearly every food chain starts with water and green plants.'

She stood up suddenly and left the room. She came back five minutes later with a faded blue exercise book in her hand. 'Here we are. That's what I did when I were a lass!'

Susie and I opened it . . .

Growing Plants

We had:
> Blotting Paper
> Saucers
> Mustard and Cress seeds
> hyacinth bulbs
> carrot tops
> Pea Seeds
> Jam jars
> Water
> Toothpicks.

What we did.

1. We soaked the blotting paper in water and sprinkled it with mustard and cress seeds

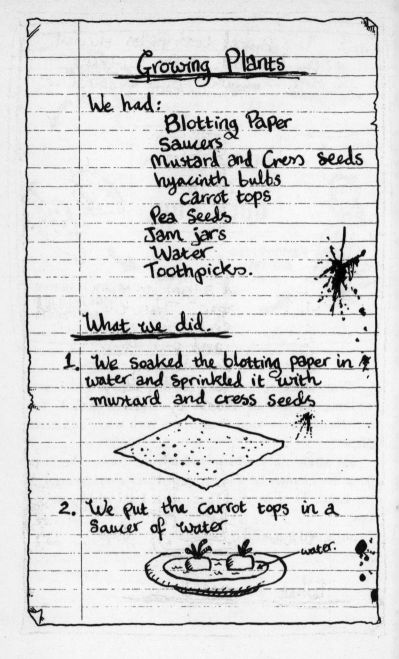

2. We put the carrot tops in a saucer of water

water.

3. We pushed tooth picks through the hyacinth bulbs so they could balance over a jam jar of water

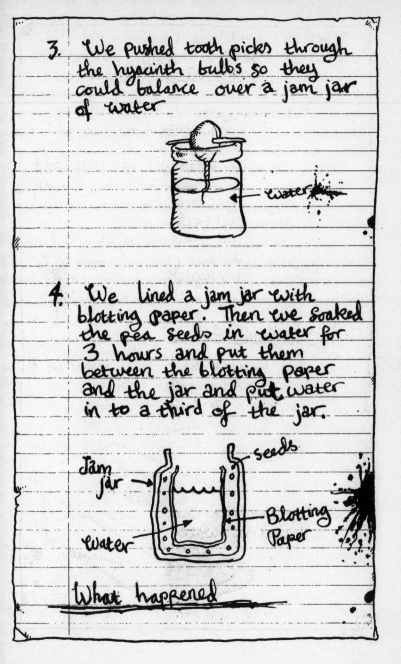

water

4. We lined a jam jar with blotting paper. Then we soaked the pea seeds in water for 3 hours and put them between the blotting paper and the jar and put water in to a third of the jar.

seeds

Jam jar →

Blotting Paper

water

What happened

'You never finished, Gran,' I said.

'No. I had to go fire-watching from the church tower the next week with my Mum. I were awake all night and skipped school all day. You'll have to try the experiment yourselves. But I do know they all grew with the roots going down to the water and the shoots going up to the light.'

'How do the carrots and things *know*?' Susie asked.

'It's nature,' Gran said. 'And another thing. Everything needs water to grow. Once they drain that swamp you kill that food chain for good.'

I was going to ask about the fire-watching but there was a sharp rap at the door. I hurried to open it. There was no one there . . . but there was a cardboard box on the doorstep and pasted on it were letters from a newspaper. They spelled out . . .

Chapter 6

I picked up the box, carried it into the kitchen and put it down on the table. Boozle, the dog, suddenly woke up and started to sniff the air.

'It must be something to eat,' Susie said. 'He only wakes up for food.'

I pushed the slobbering dog away and opened the box. Inside were two smelly kippers and a note.

FISH IN POND
WILL LUKE LIKE
THIS SOON

'Who would have sent this?' Susie asked.

'Someone who's up to no good,' Gran said. 'I think we need to go and keep an eye on the swamp tonight.'

'Why?' I asked.

'It must have been dark when that there oil was put in the swamp. I think they are planning to do something else to the water tonight. I feel it in my bones,' Gran explained.

The back door opened and Sam wandered into the kitchen whistling a stupid football song.

'One day I'm going to play for the Canaries,' he said.

'Your Grandad had a trial for them once,' Gran sighed. 'He always wanted to be a Canary. But it was never to be.'

'Wasn't he good enough,' Sam asked with interest.

'No, he kept falling off the perch,' Gran smirked.

Sam glared at her. 'I'm hungry,' he said.

'There's a couple of kippers here,' I said pointing to the box.

He peered into the box and grinned.

'Gran thinks someone is going to try and pollute the water in the swamp again,' Susie said.

'So where does the swamp water come from?' he asked casually.

'You've done about *The Water Cycle* at school,' I said impatiently.

'I was asleep that lesson,' he said.

'Look it up on the computer,' I told him. 'I've got things to do.'

I left Sam with the computer and went to fetch some blankets and a torch. If I was going to spend time in that graveyard then I needed to be warm. I collected all the things I needed and went back into the kitchen. Sam was bashing some chalk with the rolling pin.

'What are you doing?' I asked.

'Making clouds,' he said.

'Yeah, clouds of dust.'

'Look on the computer screen. It tells you how to make clouds.'

Making clouds

You need: a very large jar with a lid, crushed chalk, water, a round balloon (cut the neck off) and a thick rubber band.

1. Pour a small amount of water into the jar and put the lid on. Leave it for 20 minutes.
2. Now add some chalk powder to the water.
3. Tightly stretch the balloon over the jar and hold it on with the rubber band.
4. Press the balloon down with your fist for about 20 seconds.
5. Take off the balloon and you have made a cloud.

Pressing down on the balloon makes the air in the jar get warmer. When you take the balloon away the air cools and forms a cloud.

'Have you got everything we need?' Gran asked as she walked into the kitchen. 'Put the radio on, Sally, and let's see what the weather forecast is for tonight.'

I turned on the radio to hear the words, 'News Flash!'

WE INTERRUPT THIS PROGRAMME TO BRING YOU IMPORTANT NEWS FROM OLDCASTLE UNITED. IT HAS JUST BEEN ANNOUNCED THAT THE GREAT ROMANIAN STRIKER, SPAGELLI RAVATELLI, HAS BEEN SIGNED AS THE TEAM'S NEW STRIKER. HE HAS BEEN SUSPENDED IN ROMANIA FOR BITING AN OPPONENT ON THE NECK. WHEN ASKED IF HE WOULD CHANGE HIS WAYS WITH OLDCASTLE RAVATELLI ANSWERED, "POPPERO, LOPPERI, DOPPITY!" WHICH IS, OF COURSE, ROMANIAN FOR 'POPPERO, LOPPERI, DOPPITY!'
WE WILL BRING YOU MORE ON THIS STORY IN OUR NEXT NEWS PROGRAMME.

Sam rushed out of the kitchen shouting for Simon, 'Si, Si, you'll never believe what's happened.'

I gathered up the blankets and handed the torch to Susie. Gran carried her knitting.

It was a cold clear night and the bats were swooping overhead as we got to the swamp. We wanted to be as close to the swamp as possible but the street lights meant that there was nowhere to hide. It was no good, we would have to hide behind the graveyard wall.

We found a sheltered spot between Grandad and the wall and settled down. It had been a long and tiring day and we were starting to doze off when we heard voices.

'Great news about the new striker, Spagelli Ravatelli, Mr Racula,' said the voice of Councillor Tripewell.

'That is just the start of my great plans for Oldcastle,' came a soft and squeaky voice. 'Have you got the equipment?'

'Yes, I have the equipment. We can start tomorrow,' Councillor Timothy Tripewell said with a nasty chuckle.

Chapter 7

'I do not work in daylight,' Mr Racula said.

'Good idea,' Tripewell told him. 'Do it under the cover of darkness before those potty protesters try to stop us. I've got a couple of little helpers who'll ruin the swamp for good tonight.'

'I will have the machines brought here after dark. At midnight I will personally wipe out the swamp. By morning it will be gone with all of its foul and filthy frogs!'

Tripewell chuckled. 'You don't like frogs and fishes, then?'

'I hate all *cold*-blooded creatures,' the Oldcastle chairman hissed.

'Prefer these bats, do you?'

Mr Racula's voice was soft as a dove's, 'Oh, I just *love* these bats. They live in the tower of the church here.'

That reminded me of something. I took my 'Green Guide to Conservation' out of my pocket. I shielded the torch and shone it on the page I wanted . . .

B is for Bats

Did you know . . . bats are an endangered species? But they are now so well protected their homes can't be disturbed in any way! If you have them in your attic then you couldn't move them even if you wanted. (NOT that you would want to harm our cute and furry friends.)

Mr Racula was talking about them as if he had written the book himself. 'The bats make me feel quite at home.'

'So where are you from, Vlad Donald . . . you don't mind me calling you Vlad, do you?'

'No, Timothy. I come from Romania. A little region called Transylvania.'

'Nice part of the world, South America,' Tripewell said and turned to walk back out of the graveyard gates. He stopped. 'Oh, I nearly forgot. Do you have the money we agreed?'

The moonlight struggled through the tall trees but I could just make out the tall, cloaked shape of Mr Racula as he bent down and picked up a briefcase. 'One million pounds for getting me the planning permission. That is what we agreed.'

I heard the rasping sound of Tripewell rubbing his hands. 'And the other million when the Canaries play their first game in the new stadium.'

'It is a pleasure doing business with you,' Mr Racula said smoothly and disappeared into the deepest shadows under the church tower. We were alone.

Gran was shuffling about. 'What's wrong? Sitting on an ant-hill?' I asked.

'Let's get home! Quick!' she said.

'We have to guard the swamp!'

'This is more important,' she said and crept towards the gate, bent low and muttering, 'Bye for now, Grandad. See you tomorrow.'

The streets were quiet except for a strange rattling and rumbling that sounded like fifty supermarket trolleys being pushed over a cracked pavement in some nearby street.

When we got in the house Dad was watching television with the dog on his lap. Gran took *The Boy Scout Annual* off the bookshelves and began flicking through the pages. 'This were your Dad's when he were a lad,' Gran explained.

'I didn't know you were a Scout, Dad!' I said.

He grunted. 'For a year. Had a problem with bob-a-job week. Vicar gave me a job sweeping up leaves in the grave-yard.'

'What went wrong?' Susie asked.

'I fell out of the tree,' he sighed. 'Vicar was furious 'cos I made a hole in the grave where I landed. Shattered both legs!'

'It must have been agony!'

'Not really, the bloke'd been dead for sixty years,' Dad said shaking his head.

'Here we are!' Gran cried and showed us the page . . .

A Tracker's Guide to Footprints

Want to earn your wood-craft badge? Here's a way of spotting an animal... even when it isn't there! Make a copy of its footprint and take it back to the Scout Hut to prove it.

Be prepared with:

Strips of thick cardboard about 6 cm wide, paper clips, modelling clay, plaster of Paris, a mixing bowl and water, a wooden spoon, newspaper.

• First find your footprint.
Make a frame by pressing the cardboard strips firmly to the ground around it. Seal the joints with modelling clay and hold the strips together with paper clips.

• Put the plaster of Paris in the mixing bowl and gradually stir in water till it is thick and creamy. Make sure it has no lumps.

• Quickly pour the mixture over the footprint till the plaster is about 3 cm deep. Cover with newspaper and leave to harden for about two hours.

• Remove the plaster and you should have a clear cast of the print. Clean it carefully and paint it if you wish.

Did you know? Police use this old scout trick to catch crooks who leave footprints behind!

Remember – a Boy Scout always does his duty, so offer to help your local constable in his war against crime!

The boys burst in noisily through the front door. 'What're you up to?'

Gran explained and set about finding the materials. 'Fine, Gran,' I said. 'But why do we need a set of animal paw-prints?'

'We don't, lass,' she said with a wink that screwed up her face. 'We want to catch the crooks. We can make a cast of Councillor Tripewell's big boots next to Mr Racula's fine shoes and prove that they've been meeting in secret. That'll put a spoke in their bulldozer tracks!'

'Come on, Simon,' Sam said. 'Let's take Boozle for a walk before we go to bed!'

They vanished as quickly and noisily as they had arrived. 'Tomorrow morning, before school, we'll take those prints!' I said wearily. I went to bed, glad that we hadn't had to spend a night in that graveyard.

But next morning I wished I had. When we arrived at the swamp the sun was rising and it glinted on the bright steel shapes in the swamp. Someone had pushed about fifty supermarket trolleys in. It was a miserable mess. No one would want to save that!

And when we reached the graveyard we saw the clay path had been scratched carefully to destroy any trace of footprints from the night before.

All we could see was the print of some large animal. 'What is it?' Susie breathed.

'Some sort of monstrous hound,' I told her as we turned home for breakfast.

'What goes on here after midnight?' my sister asked, trembling a little.

'We'll find out tonight,' I said.

Chapter 8

'We have four short hours to save the swamp!' Gran said as we finished breakfast. 'From when it gets dark tonight until midnight when that Racula feller gets there.'

'We'll never do it,' Susie sighed and snivelled into her tea.

'Remember what my dad used to say,' Gran muttered. 'Never is a long time!'

I frowned. 'What does that mean?' I asked.

'I don't know . . . but it's very wise,' Gran said tapping the side of her nose. 'Now get off to school and stop worrying. When you get home I'll have thought of something. And cheer up, young Susie, you look like a wet weekend.'

'Just time to catch the local news!' Sam and Simon cried as they rushed into the room and switched on the television. 'Oldcastle are at home again tonight!'

Sure enough the reporter was interviewing the Canaries' manager . . .

The boys jumped to their feet, 'That means a new stadium in Duckpool for Oldcastle!' Simon cried and they ran out of the house chanting, 'Here we go! Here we go! Here we go! We've a new football pitch down the ro-oad!'

We tramped after them gloomily. School was miserable. SOS friends handed us their petitions but the five hundred names didn't cheer us up. What we needed was action.

We arrived home that evening and waited for darkness. Gran had a dusty old poster spread across the living-room table. She tapped it with her thin finger. 'When I were a lass this is what we did to save the countryside. We didn't know no words like "conservation" in the war. All we knew was the word "survival". But if we can clean the swamp we can make the land around it a nicer park with this!' She tapped the poster again and I looked at it . . .

HOW TO WIN THE
WAR

Top tip 27: Make your own soil

It takes nature hundreds of years to make soil. But nature doesn't have a hammer... you should! If you don't have your own garden for vegetables then make your own window-box and fill it with home-made soil. Here's how:

Take an old cotton tea towel and fill it with small rocks and stones – limestone and sandstone are best, but even a brick from a bombed out house will do!

Wrap them in the towel and beat them with a hammer till they're crushed to grains like sugar.

Add an equal amount of peat moss from your local hardware shop.

Add plant leftovers – potato skins, fruit peel, tea leaves and even egg shells if you've been lucky enough to have an egg!

Add water and mix. Plant bean seeds and leave them in the sun to grow.

Remember –
Every little helps!

'Was it really that bad in the war?' I asked.

'We made do,' Gran said. 'It was the bombing that really scared us. I used to go to the churchyard and climb the church tower with my Mam – your great-gran. We'd spend all night watching for fire bombs landing. I had to run with a message to the fire station when I saw one. Remember not many people had telephones in them days.'

'Wasn't it spooky?' Susie asked.

'Only when the old bell rang,' Gran said in a low voice. 'They reckoned there were a ghost in that there graveyard. When someone were due to be hit with a bomb, the ghost would ring the old bell! Thirteen bongs! A warning of doom!'

'Did you ever hear it?' a voice behind me asked. I have to admit I jumped a little. But it was only simple Simon.

'When the wind were howling through the tower it would stir the bell and make it ring. Then the bats would get excited and fly around. It were like black confetti at a wedding!' Gran said and her voice creaked like the old church gate.

'I've never heard it,' Simon said. 'And I've fished for tadpoles at the swamp on some pretty windy days.'

'You wouldn't, lad! They took the bell away and melted it down to make guns and things in 1945. It was never replaced. That tower's as silent as the graves below and now the bats can sleep in peace.'

Simon nodded thoughtfully and went upstairs to his room, calling, 'Sam! Time to go to the match! The Canaries are playing Beestley Villa!'

Susie, Gran and I looked out of the window. It was dark. It was time!

Chapter 9

'Are you ready then, girls?' Gran asked. 'Shall we go and save that there swamp?'

'What are we going to do?' Susie and I asked together.

'Get all the trolleys out,' Gran said.

'But that will take hours,' Susie moaned.

'Not with a bulldozer,' Gran grinned.

We grabbed our coats and shut the front door quietly behind us. When we reached the swamp the trolleys looked like metal branches growing out of the water. The real branches of the old dead tree hung over them like a giant black claw. Gran took one look at the bulldozer and clambered into the driver's seat.

'Gran, do you know what you are doing?' I asked.

'It's just like driving a car,' she replied. 'Only more fun.

And you don't get no road-ragers arguing with you!'

The roar of the bulldozer engine filled the air and Gran was off on her mission to clear the swamp. Susie and I could only watch in amazement. She scooped the first load of trolleys out of the water without even touching the trees on either side. Then she turned the bulldozer round and drove away.

'Where's she going?' Susie asked.

'I've no idea.'

A few minutes later the bulldozer rumbled back with an empty bucket. Gran took away five more loads before the swamp was clear. She parked the bulldozer on a patch of wasteland and climbed out. She was grinning all over her face. 'Let's collect a water sample to show how clean it is now,' she suggested and I gathered some in an empty lemonade bottle I'd brought.

'Where did you put the trolleys?' Susie asked.

'I took them and dumped them in somebody's front garden.'

'That's dreadful!' Susie cried.

Gran shrugged. 'Depends whose garden it is, doesn't it?' was all she would say.

'Come on, we need to hide before Mr Racula gets here,' I said.

'We've got ages yet. I just need to nobble the bulldozer,' Gran said. 'We don't want anyone using it to damage the swamp again tonight.' She tugged a few wires loose. 'There! It'll fix easy enough in daylight.'

As we walked to the graveyard I noticed that the bats were busily flying to and fro.

'It's amazing how they never bang into anything,' I said.

'We play a game at Guides called *Being A Bat*,' Susie piped up.

'I love games,' Gran said. 'Show me how to be a bat. Grandad will enjoy this.'

'OK. Bats squeak at things – like a moth. They work out how far away it is by listening for the echo,' Susie explained.

Gran squeaked and flapped her arms like a bat.

I looked round to see Gran tripping round the grave-yard tapping a stick on the ground.

'Oooops, sorry Grandad,' she said, bouncing off his gravestone.

'Come on, Gran,' I said, 'it's time we hid.'

'Did you bring the radio?' she asked.

'Yes. Why?'

'Just turn it on for a minute. We'd better check that there haven't been any new developments from Councillor Tripewell and his friends.'

I turned on the pocket radio and tuned in to the local radio channel.

AND HERE IS TONIGHT'S AMAZING FOOTBALL RESULT: OLDCASTLE UNITED O – BEESTLEY VILLA 10. WE GO OVER TO OUR REPORTER AT THE GROUND FOR HIS REPORT ON THIS TERRIBLE SCORE FOR THE CANARIES...

NEW SIGNING, SPAGELLI RAVATELLI, SCORED TEN OWN GOALS TO SHATTER OLDCASTLE. WHEN HIS TEAM MATES TRIED TO STOP HIM SCORING NUMBER 11 HE BIT SEVERAL OF THEM ON THE NECK BEFORE BEING SENT OFF FOR UNGENTLEMANLY BEHAVIOUR. MANAGER KEN GODDLE SAID "IT COULD HAVE BEEN WORSE...

'Turn it off!' hissed Gran. 'There's someone coming.'

I turned the radio off and peered over the wall. Gran was right. She may not be a very good bat but her hearing was better than mine.

Although the moon was covered by a cloud, I could still make out the fat figure of Councillor Tripewell walking towards the graveyard.

'Keep your eyes and ears peeled,' Gran whispered. 'That huge hound may be prowling the graveyard!'

'Or the vampire!' Susie whimpered.

We crouched down below the wall and waited. Then
... *DONG-G-G-G-G-G!*

The sound of the church bell rang through the night air.
It struck thirteen.

Chapter 10

A blood-chilling scream came from the shadow of the church tower. The bat-shaped form of Mr Donald Racula raced towards the gate where he collided with Councillor Tripewell. The booming sound terrified the bats too and they blotted out the moon as they fled from their home in the tower.

'The bells! The bells!' the bat-cloaked man cried.

'What about them?' Tripewell roared.

'When the phantom bell rings it's a certain sign that someone will die before the night is out!' Mr Racula moaned.

'What are you worried about, man? You're not Donald Racula . . . you are Count Dracula of the Undead!'

'No, I'm not. I'm Donald Racula of Unstead! Dressing up like this and changing my name was just my hobby. Ever since I saw the film. I'm a vegetarian, actually! I married a Romanian, you know, but she left me and went back home. Now I spend my money on football and my

nights wandering in graveyards, dressed like my vampire
bat hero.'

'I can't cope with your problems now, Racula. We have
more than bats and bells to worry about!'

'More than the *phantom* bell? What could be worse,
Timothy?'

'Your football team were trounced tonight, ten–nil.
That son of yours scored ten own-goals! He's as much use
as an ashtray on a motorbike!'

'Ah, little Spagelli Ravatelli Racula . . . his mother
named him after her favourite ballroom dancer – he's been
living with her in Romania, you know. He does go a bit
funny when it's a full moon.'

'He's not the only one. I came past my house on the
way here from the match and some idiot's piled fifty shopping trolleys in my front garden!' Councillor Tripewell

sighed. 'We'll never get into the Premier League at this rate. Get that swamp dug up now before the SOS nutters stop us!'

The two men left the churchyard. The great phantom bell had faded to silence. 'Gran,' I whispered. 'We have to stop them.'

'Heh! Heh!' she chuckled. 'No we don't. 'I've taken the rotor arm out of the bulldozer. It'll never start. We have another twelve hours. Tomorrow morning we'll show the world how clean the swamp really is.'

Back home we found Dad watching television gloomily.

WELL GLEN, YOU LOOK REMARKABLY HAPPY FOR A MANAGER WHOSE TEAM HAS JUST LOST TEN-NIL!

AYE! I HAD A BET ON THAT OLDCASTLE WOULD LOSE TEN NIL. I'VE WON A MILLION POUNDS!

YOU'LL BE SACKED!

WITH A MILLION POUNDS IN MY POCKET, I DON'T CARE!

'Always thought there was something funny about that bloke,' Dad sighed. He stood up, picked up a bottle from the table and poured himself a drink.

Suddenly he clutched his throat, gave a gurgling, gasping, choking cry and fell to his knees. 'Poison! That lemonade's been poisoned.'

'The phantom bell!' Susie gasped. 'Dad! You are the one that's fated to die!'

Gran snatched the bottle from him. 'That's our sample of pond water. It's a bit muddy but it won't hurt you, son. Get up, you soft lump. You'll live.'

The front door opened and our brothers walked in. 'What're you doing on the floor, Dad?'

'Dying!'

'Don't people usually do that in bed?' Simon asked.

'What was the football score?' Sam asked.

'I thought you'd been to the match,' I said sharply.

'Yeah,' Sam muttered. The boys looked at one another and hurried up the stairs to their room while Dad staggered back to his chair and sat down.

Gran led the way into the kitchen. 'What we need to do is sort the mud from the water. I churned it up a bit with me bulldozing.'

'How do we do that?' I asked.

'That was another thing we learned during the war,' Gran said and pulled out her notebook.

Pure Water Wins Wars!

Teacher said that all this bombing can break pipes and send us muddy water through the taps. Boiling it will make it safe but it still looks really horrible. So this is how to make fresh water.

We had: a large pan, a glass shorter than the pan, 2 small clean stones, a piece of plastic food wrap big enough to fit over the pan, sticky tape.

1. We poured about 5cm of the muddy water into the pan.

2. We put the glass in the middle of the water and put a stone in to stop it floating about.

3. We covered the pan with clear plastic, pulled it tight and taped the sides to the pan.

4. We put the second stone on the plastic over the glass, but didn't let the plastic touch the glass. Then we put the whole lot in warm sunlight.

PTO

73

We didn't have any sunlight and the moonlight wouldn't work. So we left the experiment near the radiator and went to bed. I was a long time going to sleep, mainly because Susie was snivelling. 'Sally!'

'What?'

'It could be *me* that's going to die! I was one of the ones to hear the phantom bell! It could be me! I could wake up dead!'

'You could,' I agreed.

'Ooooh! How do you think I'm going to die?'

'Your big sister is going to batter you to death with a pillow because you won't shut up.'

Susie shut up.

74

Chapter 11

At lunchtime next day, Susie and I raced out of school and round to the swamp.

Gran was already there and was surrounded by reporters and photographers. She was arguing with Councillor Tripewell.

In one hand she held a bottle of clear water. In the other she held the morning paper with the dramatic headlines . . .

OLDCASTLE OUT!

Following last night's betting scandal, Oldcastle
United have been banned from the football league.
Manager Ken Goddle bet on his team to lose 10–0,
which they did. A spokesperson for the football
league said, 'If there's any fixing going to be done
then we'll do it.'

Fans of Oldcastle, known as the Canaries, were
stunned by the news. There is no team for them to
support and plans for a super-stadium seem point-
less now.

Councillor Tripewell was sitting behind the controls of
a bulldozer. His hair was wild and his eyes bulging like
well-licked gob-stoppers. 'You interfering busybodies can
just clear out of the way. I've got planning permission!' He
waved a paper back at Gran. 'I'm building a stadium even
if there's no one to play in it!'

'Over my dead body!' Gran shouted while the crowds
cheered.

'And mine!' I said, jumping to her side.

The sound of the bulldozer engine cut through the air.
Tripewell crashed it into gear and it edged forward, huge
and yellow as a banana . . . but harder and deadlier.

The reporters who had seen their story slipping away
suddenly became interested again. I could see the headline:

FINAL SCORE FROM OLDCASTLE: GRAN 0 - BULLDOZER 1

The battle to build the new football stadium took a dramatic turn today. As the bulldozers rolled in to clear the land known as The Swamp, Mrs Gertrude Spark stepped out in front of them. It was a brave, fearless and stupid gesture. She was taken to the general hospital but . . .

'Sally!' Susie's voice snapped me out of my day-dream. 'Look, the noise has disturbed the bats. They're flying out of the tree.'

'You mean the bats are in the tree!' I shouted.

'Well, at the moment they're flying around it.'

'Get a picture of those bats,' one reporter called. 'It'll make a great story. *Bats booted out in battle.*'

'You can't do that,' I shouted.

'You mean we can't take a photograph?' asked the reporter.

'Not you,' I said and pointed to the bulldozer. 'He can't knock down the bats' home. He's not allowed to.'

'I've got planning permission!' Tripewell roared over the sound of the engine. 'I can do what I want with this land.'

'You can dig up all the land apart from that tree,' I said calmly. 'You are *not* allowed to move bats. They are a protected animal and it's against the law to touch them or their homes.'

'She's right,' said the reporter. 'I did a story on them last year. Lovely couple had some bats move into their loft and there was nothing they could do about it.'

Our local Police Constable pulled his helmet down and stepped forward. 'Sorry, sir, I'll have to ask you to cease and desist. Bulldoze a bat and I'll bang you up behind bars!'

Councillor Tripewell went a strange shade of purple, pointed to Gran and screamed, 'This is all her fault.' He put his foot down till the machine's engine was screaming and drove straight towards Gran. Gran turned to face him and looked him straight in the eye. She wasn't going to

move. My Gran was going to get crushed.

'Gran's to be the victim of the phantom bell!' Susie screamed. 'I knew it had to be somebody!'

Gran held the newspaper in front of her the way a matador holds his cape in a bullfight. They'd never seen a bulldozer fight in Duckpool till that day. Just as the madman was about to hit her, she jinked sideways.

It was too late for Tripewell to change his direction and he thundered on to the road and straight over the reporters' parked cars. There was chaos as the reporters attacked the councillor and the photographers tried to take pictures.

It was when he tried to run over a double-decker bus that Tripewell met his match and ground to a halt. The

constable stepped on to the cab and led the sobbing Tripewell away.

'Well, that's a good day's work done. I think it's time for a cup of tea,' said Gran as it started to rain. 'And when we get home I'll show you how to make rain,' she said staring at the sky.

'You're not going to do that rain dance again, are you?' I asked.

'Wait and see,' she grinned.

We walked into the house just as the rain started to pour down. I walked into the kitchen and put the kettle on. Gran picked up a large metal spoon, put it in the freezer and went upstairs.

How to Confuse your Dog
Make it rain indoors

① Take a large metal spoon or ladle and put it in the freezer

② Fill the kettle about ¼ full and turn it on.

A few minutes later she came into the kitchen with a leaflet. 'Try this,' she said. I took the leaflet and followed the instructions.

'Boozle,' Susie shouted. 'Biccies.'

Boozle hurtled through the kitchen door and slid on the patch of rain. He crashed into the cupboards and landed on Sam's school bag under the table. The dog definitely looked confused.

Susie went to stroke the dozy animal but when it rolled on to the bag the sound of a church bell rang out from under the table. It struck thirteen.

'The phantom bell!' she gasped.

But Gran was looking at the dog's wet footprint on the

③ CLACK When the kettle boils get the spoon out of the freezer and hold it in the steam.

④ You will see 'rain' falling from the spoon. It works because the cold spoon cools the water vapour coming from the kettle. It changes back into water and falls like rain.

⑤ Call your dog and see what happens...

I'M CONFUSED! WEIRD! SPOOKY!

floor. 'Where have we seen *that* before?' she asked. Her mouth was set in a grim line.

Councillor Tripewell had been defeated. But there was trouble in store for someone else.

Chapter 12

When we arrived home after school that evening, Gran called us all into the kitchen for tea. As a pan of spaghetti simmered on the cooker she lifted a shoe box off the table.

'What's that, Gran?' Simon asked.
'Nothing you'd be interested in,' she said.
'We are, aren't we, Sam?' Simon insisted.
Gran shrugged and put the box on the table. 'It was

something that Councillor Tripewell said about his wormery. It reminded me of this experiment I used to do at school . . .'

FIRST I GATHERED EVERYTHING ON THE TABLE

PAPER TOWELS

TAP WATER

SHOEBOX

NOTEBOOK PAPER

STICKY TAPE

SCISSORS

A TORCH

I TAPED THE NOTEBOOK PAPER INSIDE THE LID OF THE BOX SO THAT IT WOULD HANG A COUPLE OF CENTIMETRES OFF THE BOTTOM WHEN THE LID WAS ON. I CUT A HOLE IN ONE END OF THE LID, A LITTLE SMALLER THAN THE TORCH

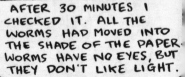

I PUT MOISTENED PAPER TOWELS ON THE BOTTOM OF THE BOX AND PUT THE EARTHWORMS AT THE END WITH THE HOLE. I PUT THE TORCH OVER THE HOLE AND SWITCHED IT ON...

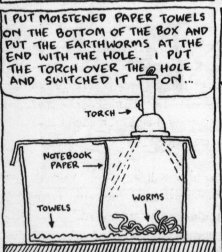

TORCH →

NOTEBOOK PAPER →

TOWELS

WORMS

AFTER 30 MINUTES I CHECKED IT. ALL THE WORMS HAD MOVED INTO THE SHADE OF THE PAPER. WORMS HAVE NO EYES, BUT THEY DON'T LIKE LIGHT.

'Let's see the worms then,' Sam said.

'I buried them in the garden when I'd finished,' Gran said.

The boys looked disappointed. They would do.

Gran served the spaghetti on toast and, as the boys ate, she said, 'That Councillor Tripewell didn't do all those wicked things himself, you know.'

The boys shovelled spaghetti into their mouths and kept their eyes down.

I agreed. 'Once we started our SOS campaign we were followed. Someone was out to stop us! Someone who wanted to see Oldcastle playing in a new Duckpool stadium!'

'We were followed right from the start,' Susie said. 'That can't have been Tripewell.'

'So who followed us?' I asked.

'Who poured oil into the swamp?' Susie added.

'Who left that kipper on our doorstep with the threatening letter?'

'And who signed stupid names on the petition?'

'Who dumped those supermarket trolleys in the swamp?' I asked. 'Can you tell us, Gran?'

'The same people that scratched out the footprints before we could make a mould. The same people that took a tape recorder to the top of the church tower and played a phantom bell to scare us off!' Gran said and her eyes were bullet-hard.

'We'll never prove anything now, will we, Gran?' I asked.

'The villains made just two mistakes,' she said. 'First, they left their own footprint clue at the graveyard.'

'The monster hound?' Susie asked.

'A hound that also left the same paw-print on our kitchen floor half an hour ago.'

'Boozle! Our Boozle was with the villains?' I nodded and my eyes turned to follow Gran's stony stare.

'And, of course,' she went on, 'they left the tape with the phantom bell in one of their school bags. It clicked on by accident earlier this evening.'

Susie turned her eyes on our brothers. 'It was Sam and Simon all along.'

They looked up guiltily. 'What are you going to do?'

'Nothing,' Gran said.

'Nothing?'

'Nothing . . . so long as you join the SOS team in tidying up the swamp this weekend.'

The boys nodded eagerly. Glad to be getting off so lightly. 'Anyway, that bell drove the bats from the tower to the hollow tree,' Gran told them. 'It's thanks to *you* we saved the swamp!' The boys looked gloomy – Susie and I tried not to look smug. It was hard. 'That's settled, then,' Gran said. 'Now I can enjoy my tea.' She turned to the kitchen work-top, put her hand on a tin of spaghetti and gave a small cry.

'What's wrong, Gran?' Simon asked.

She clutched her throat in horror. 'This spaghetti tin – it's *full*! Yet I just gave you a pan of the stuff!'

'You can't have given them *spaghetti* then, Gran,' I said.

Simon's mouth smiled nervously. 'Of course she did!'

'Are you *quite* sure you buried those worms in the garden, Gran?' Susie asked.

'Now you mention it,' Gran said. 'I can't remember burying them at all! Eeeeh! I do hope I didn't pop worms into the saucepan instead of the spaghetti . . .'

But she never finished. The chairs clattered to the floor as Sam and Simon raced one another to the bathroom door. Half an hour later they were still being sick.

'They had spaghetti, Gran,' I said.

'They *did*,' she said. 'But sometimes really bad children need a little extra punishment.' She smiled. 'Let's go and watch television.'

The local news came on

OLDCASTLE UNITED ARE FINISHED. BUT A NEW TEAM WILL BE FORMED AT THE DUCKPOOL ARMS INN TO PLAY ON THE OLDCASTLE PITCH. THEY WILL TRY TO GET THIS COMPLETELY NEW TEAM BACK INTO THE FOOTBALL LEAGUE NEXT SEASON. I HAVE HERE THE ORGANIZER OF THE NEW TEAM. WHAT CAN YOU TELL ME ABOUT THEM, MR SPARK?

'Dad!' we all cried as his ugly face flashed on to the screen.

Of course! Good old Dad.

**Here is a list of the experiments in this book.
Have you tried them all?**